The Tiny Little Christmas Tree

Printed and bound in the United States of America
First printing • ISBN 978-1-7328939-0-0
Copyright © 2018

TO ORDER ADDITIONAL COPIES OF:

The Tiny Little Christmas Tree

VISIT:
WWW.SCOTTPUBLISHINGCOMPANY.COM/STORE

SCOTT COMPANY PUBLISHING
CHILDREN'S BOOK DIVISION
P.O. Box 9707 • Kalispell, MT 59904
Toll Free: 1-800-628-0212
Fax: 1-406-756-0098

We dedicate this book to our loving parents:

John "Jack" & Edith Langtry O'Neill

and

William "Bumpy" & Meta Mencken Oliver

with all our love forever.

Thanks for the memories...

As he sat looking out the window of his log home, the little boy named Oliver had his best friends next to him...Prancer, Vixen and Cupid. He thought they looked like reindeer without antlers as they were Golden Retrievers.

It was snowing and beautiful-the snow sticking to the branches of the trees-the pine trees looked almost white like snow ghosts. While staring out the window the trees began to disappear and huge mounds of snow began to form.

2

As Oliver continued his watch of the snow piling up, the two trees closest to him were the Mom and Dad trees. His full attention was on the little tree about 200 feet away. When he was about 3 years old, the "Daddy" tree was dug up roots and all, bundled, and brought into the house for Christmas. Afterwards it was carefully taken care of and in the spring replanted in front of the house. Two years later the "Mommy" tree was dug up and brought into the house for Christmas as well. Now with both the Mommy and Daddy trees out front, his gaze was upon the "Baby" tree still out in the meadow. He remembered asking his mom and dad to bring the little tree in this year. They both told him that "Baby" was too small. He tried to convince them that he was little, too, and had his family with him, and the Mommy and Daddy trees wanted their whole family together as well.

4

As Oliver looked out towards the forest and across the meadow, he saw movement. It was a horse-drawn sleigh with red bows and bells with his mother and father huddled in the front seat. Bundled up against the bitter cold and blowing snow, you could barely see their faces. That was how you dressed for winter in Montana. Prancer, Vixen and Cupid were excited and walking back and forth, "talking" to each other while nuzzling with enthusiasm.

The smile on Oliver's face was wonderful as Christmas was near. The red bows and the sound of bells excited him to no end. He wanted the little tree to be with them for Christmas as this is what Christmas is about... Family.

7

When Mom and Dad arrived, hugs and kisses were given and then all had chores to do. When they were out of sight, Oliver, Prancer, Vixen and Cupid snuck up to the Christmas box in the attic. Oliver opened it and gazed at all the Christmas colors. There it was-he found it-the beautiful Angel holding a star. She was dressed in white with blond silky hair, holding the star in the dim light of the attic. This would be the first ornament for Little Tree. He found a small box, put the Angel and star in it and went to the front door. All four of them went outside, and Prancer, Vixon and Cupid couldn't wait as they bounded off into the snow to play.

8

While they were having fun and completely snow covered, Oliver went to his baby tree. He took the Angel out of the box, put the box on the ground, and stood on it. Just tall enough, he stretched and put the beautiful ornament on the very top branch. It was magical as he stepped off the box and gazed at Little Tree with the Angel on top.

As light was fading, the tree seemed to have its own sparkle with the snow coming down covering the branches and the Angel with the star. Oliver was so proud and excited. He had done it, now to convince his mom and dad as only a little boy can do. This was going to be the first Christmas with his new friend.

As his mom was preparing dinner, Prancer, Vixen and Cupid were cleaning their snow encrusted paws. Oliver stood on his personal stool and helped her with dinner. His daydreams were taking him to the baby tree that he wanted to be in their house for Christmas. He closed his eyes and could almost see Little Tree inside, in the Christmas room ready to be decorated.

When the family sat at the dinner table, Prancer, Vixen and Cupid were at his side

13

waiting for the snacks they were sure to get. As Oliver ate dinner, he looked at his mom and dad and said, "The little tree is like me, he wants to be with his family. Pleeeeeeease let this be my present!" His parents looked at each other and simultaneously said, "Yes!" Oliver looked back and forth at both of them and with tears of happiness on his face, smiled the largest smile. This was his Christmas.

15

Outside the snowstorm increased into almost a whiteout and Oliver, as hard as he tried, could barely make out the little tree with the angel and star. He was so excited that he went to the mudroom to get a shovel for his dad and wanted to go outside right then, but Dad said no because it was bedtime. Just before bedtime the snowstorm stopped and he begged his dad again, "Let's go!"
Dad just could not say no, and off they went along with the faithful trio-Prancer, Vixen and Cupid-all looking forward to playing chase and rolling in the snow like a snowball.

They got to the little tree with their faithful "American Flyer" sled and put the shovel to the ground only to find it frozen. Dad kept trying while the puppies helped by digging with their paws, and found it was only frozen a few inches down. They dug the hole with the puppies playing nearby. They thought playing was more important than work. The three of them were covered in snow and appeared as ghosts in the night. When they finished digging the dirt around the tree, Dad and Oliver put it on the sled and pulled it over the snow hills toward the house. All five of them, covered with snow and cold, brought Little Tree home. The tree was covered too, but somehow the Angel with the star on top sparkled in the moonlight.

When they reached the mudroom, Dad and Oliver shook the snow off their clothes and put the tree inside to defrost. The pups shook so hard that snow was flying everywhere.

Tomorrow was the big day-Christmas was fast approaching and they had decorating to do. Right after breakfast they carried Little Tree to the Christmas room to be decorated. The tree was beautiful by itself, but as the lights went on the beauty of the moment increased. The decorations of Christmas past were put on the branches and the lights reflected off them, making the Angel holding the star shine even brighter. It was a tradition for each dog to bring a box of ornaments to be placed upon the tree. The oldest dog taught the younger pups how to carefully carry them without breaking. The best part was that Little Tree would begin its new life in the Spring with its Mom and Dad in the yard outside the window. Life would soon begin anew with nature and a special bonding between both the families.

19

The End

About the Authors

Meta Mencken Oliver O'Neill, "Mimi" was born in Charleston, SC, and lived there her entire life until 14 year ago when she married her husband, Doug O'Neill. She is a retired surgical nurse, photographer and an avid baker; a mother and a grandmother. Currently, Mimi is in the process of writing a solo cookbook.

John Douglas O'Neill, "Doug" was born in Evanston, Illinois, and has lived in numerous places. He is retired from sales and he is a father and grandfather. Mimi and Doug now live in Kila, Montana, and are the owners of two amazing Golden Retrievers. Together, they have co-authored this book. They hope you enjoy reading it with your families as much as they have enjoyed writing it!

Acknowledgements

A special thanks to Shane Morgan, our gifted illustrator, who was a delight to work with. Thanks to our talented publisher, Scott Graber, who guided us through the process of publishing our first book. Also, special "kudos" to all who shared their unique gifts and talents and were a part of breathing life into our dream! And last, but not least, thanks to my grandson, Evan, who was the inspiration for the character, Oliver!